THIS BOOK BELONGS TO:

Date

Location ....

Time ....
AM/PM

Hunting
Partner(s) ....

Weather Conditions

....

Moon Phase

....

Terrain

....

Time	Species	Size	Seen	Shot	Lost	Cap-tured

Wildlife Sightings

Gear/Set Up

Notes

Photos

Date

Location ....

Time .... **Hunting Partner(s)** ....

AM/PM

Weather Conditions

Moon Phase

Terrain

Time	Species	Size	Seen	Shot	Lost	Cap-tured

Wildlife Sightings

Gear/Set Up

Notes

Photos

Date

Location ....

Time .... AM/PM

Hunting Partner(s) ....

Weather Conditions

Moon Phase

Terrain

Time	Species	Size	Seen	Shot	Lost	Captured

Wildlife Sightings

Gear/Set Up

Notes

Photos

Date

Location

Time

AM/PM

Hunting Partner(s)

Weather Conditions

Moon Phase

Terrain

Time	Species	Size	Seen	Shot	Lost	Cap-tured

Wildlife Sightings

Gear/Set Up

Notes

Photos

Date

Location

Time   AM/PM

Hunting
Partner(s)

Weather Conditions

Moon Phase

Terrain

Time	Species	Size	Seen	Shot	Lost	Cap-tured

Wildlife Sightings

Gear/Set Up

Notes

Photos

Date

Location

Time _____ AM/PM   Hunting Partner(s)

Weather Conditions

Moon Phase

Terrain

Time	Species	Size	Seen	Shot	Lost	Captured

Wildlife Sightings

Gear/Set Up

Notes

Photos

Date

Location ....

Time .... Hunting ....
AM/PM Partner(s)

Weather Conditions

Moon Phase

Terrain

Time	Species	Size	Seen	Shot	Lost	Cap-tured

Wildlife Sightings

Gear/Set Up

Notes

Photos

Date

Location _____

Time _____ Hunting Partner(s) _____

AM/PM

Weather Conditions

Moon Phase

Terrain

Time	Species	Size	Seen	Shot	Lost	Cap-tured

Wildlife Sightings

Gear/Set Up

Notes

Photos

Date

Location ....

Time .... Hunting
       AM/PM   Partner(s) ....

Weather Conditions

....

Moon Phase

....

Terrain

....

Time	Species	Size	Seen	Shot	Lost	Cap-tured

Wildlife Sightings

Gear/Set Up

Notes

Photos

Date

Location

Time .... AM/PM

Hunting Partner(s)

Weather Conditions

Moon Phase

Terrain

Time	Species	Size	Seen	Shot	Lost	Cap-tured

Wildlife Sightings

Gear/Set Up

Notes

Photos

Date

Location

Time   Hunting
         AM/PM   Partner(s)

Weather Conditions

Moon Phase

Terrain

Time	Species	Size	Seen	Shot	Lost	Cap-tured

Wildlife Sightings

Gear/Set Up

Notes

Photos

Date

Location ....

Time .... **Hunting Partner(s)** ....
AM/PM

Weather Conditions

....

Moon Phase

....

Terrain

....

Time	Species	Size	Seen	Shot	Lost	Cap-tured

Wildlife Sightings

Gear/Set Up

Notes

Photos

Date

Location ....

Time _____ Hunting ....
AM/PM Partner(s)

Weather Conditions

Moon Phase

Terrain

Time	Species	Size	Seen	Shot	Lost	Cap-tured

Wildlife Sightings

Gear/Set Up

Notes

Photos

Date

Location _____

Time _____ AM/PM   Hunting Partner(s) _____

Weather Conditions

Moon Phase

Terrain

Time	Species	Size	Seen	Shot	Lost	Cap-tured

Wildlife Sightings

Gear/Set Up

Notes

Photos

Date

Location

Time .... AM/PM

Hunting Partner(s)

Weather Conditions

Moon Phase

Terrain

Time	Species	Size	Seen	Shot	Lost	Cap-tured

Wildlife Sightings

Gear/Set Up

Notes

Photos

Date

Location

Time

AM/PM

Hunting
Partner(s)

Weather Conditions

Moon Phase

Terrain

Time	Species	Size	Seen	Shot	Lost	Cap-tured

Wildlife Sightings

Gear/Set Up

Notes

Photos

Date

Location ....

Time .... AM/PM

Hunting Partner(s) ....

Weather Conditions

....

Moon Phase

....

Terrain

....

Time	Species	Size	Seen	Shot	Lost	Cap-tured

Wildlife Sightings

Gear/Set Up

Notes

Photos

Date

Location

Time

AM/PM

Hunting Partner(s)

Weather Conditions

Moon Phase

Terrain

Time	Species	Size	Seen	Shot	Lost	Cap-tured

Wildlife Sightings

Gear/Set Up

Notes

Photos

Date

Location

Time _____ AM/PM

Hunting Partner(s) _____

Weather Conditions

Moon Phase

Terrain

Time	Species	Size	Seen	Shot	Lost	Cap-tured

Wildlife Sightings

Gear/Set Up

Notes

Photos

Date

Location

Time _____ AM/PM

Hunting Partner(s) _____

Weather Conditions

Moon Phase

Terrain

Time	Species	Size	Seen	Shot	Lost	Cap-tured

Wildlife Sightings

Gear/Set Up

Notes

Photos

Date

Location

Time ___ AM/PM   Hunting Partner(s)

Weather Conditions

Moon Phase

Terrain

Time	Species	Size	Seen	Shot	Lost	Cap-tured

Wildlife Sightings

Gear/Set Up

Notes

Photos

Date

Location _____

Time _____ AM/PM

Hunting
Partner(s) _____

Weather Conditions

Moon Phase

Terrain

Time	Species	Size	Seen	Shot	Lost	Cap-tured

Wildlife Sightings

Gear/Set Up

Notes

Photos

Date

Location	
Time	
	AM/PM

Hunting
Partner(s)

Weather Conditions

Moon Phase

Terrain

Time	Species	Size	Seen	Shot	Lost	Cap-tured

Wildlife Sightings

Gear/Set Up

Notes

Photos

Date

Location

Time _____ AM/PM   Hunting Partner(s)

Weather Conditions

Moon Phase

Terrain

Time	Species	Size	Seen	Shot	Lost	Cap-tured

Wildlife Sightings

Gear/Set Up

Notes

Photos

Date

Location

Time _____ / AM/PM

Hunting Partner(s)

Weather Conditions

Moon Phase

Terrain

Time	Species	Size	Seen	Shot	Lost	Cap-tured

Wildlife Sightings

Gear/Set Up

Notes

Date

Location

Time

AM/PM

Hunting
Partner(s)

Weather Conditions

Moon Phase

Terrain

Time	Species	Size	Seen	Shot	Lost	Cap-tured

Wildlife Sightings

Gear/Set Up

Notes

Photos

Date

Location	
Time	
	AM/PM
Hunting Partner(s)	

Weather Conditions

Moon Phase

Terrain

Time	Species	Size	Seen	Shot	Lost	Cap-tured

Wildlife Sightings

Gear/Set Up

Notes

Photos

Date

Location

Time _____ AM/PM

Hunting Partner(s)

Weather Conditions

Moon Phase

Terrain

Time	Species	Size	Seen	Shot	Lost	Cap-tured

Wildlife Sightings

Gear/Set Up

Notes

Date

Location

Time _____ AM/PM

Hunting Partner(s)

Weather Conditions

Moon Phase

Terrain

Time	Species	Size	Seen	Shot	Lost	Cap-tured

Wildlife Sightings

Gear/Set Up

Notes

Date

Location _____

Time _____ Hunting
        AM/PM   Partner(s) _____

Weather Conditions

Moon Phase

Terrain

Time	Species	Size	Seen	Shot	Lost	Cap-tured

Wildlife Sightings

Gear/Set Up

Notes

Photos

Date

Location	
Time	
	AM/PM

Hunting Partner(s)

Weather Conditions

Moon Phase

Terrain

Time	Species	Size	Seen	Shot	Lost	Cap-tured

Wildlife Sightings

Gear/Set Up

Notes

Date

Location ....

Time .... Hunting
AM/PM Partner(s) ....

Weather Conditions

Moon Phase

Terrain

Time	Species	Size	Seen	Shot	Lost	Cap-tured

Wildlife Sightings

Gear/Set Up

Notes

Photos

Date

Location

Time _____ AM/PM

Hunting Partner(s) _____

Weather Conditions

Moon Phase

Terrain

Time	Species	Size	Seen	Shot	Lost	Cap-tured

Wildlife Sightings

Gear/Set Up

Notes

Photos

Date

Location

Time _____

AM/PM

Hunting Partner(s)

Weather Conditions

Moon Phase

Terrain

Time	Species	Size	Seen	Shot	Lost	Cap-tured

Wildlife Sightings

Gear/Set Up

Notes

Photos

Date

Location _____

Time _____ AM/PM

Hunting Partner(s) _____

Weather Conditions

_____

Moon Phase

_____

Terrain

_____

Time	Species	Size	Seen	Shot	Lost	Cap-tured

Wildlife Sightings

Gear/Set Up

Notes

Photos

Date

Location ....

Time _____   AM/PM   Hunting Partner(s) _____

Weather Conditions

Moon Phase

Terrain

Time	Species	Size	Seen	Shot	Lost	Cap-tured

Wildlife Sightings

Gear/Set Up

Notes

Date

Location

Time

AM/PM

Hunting
Partner(s)

Weather Conditions

Moon Phase

Terrain

Time	Species	Size	Seen	Shot	Lost	Cap-tured

Wildlife Sightings

Gear/Set Up

Notes

Photos

Date

Location _____

Time _____ AM/PM

Hunting Partner(s) _____

Weather Conditions

Moon Phase

Terrain

Time	Species	Size	Seen	Shot	Lost	Cap-tured

Wildlife Sightings

Gear/Set Up

Notes

Date

Location	
Time	
	AM/PM

Hunting
Partner(s)

Weather Conditions

Moon Phase

Terrain

Time	Species	Size	Seen	Shot	Lost	Cap-tured

Wildlife Sightings

Gear/Set Up

Notes

Photos

Made in the USA
Columbia, SC
15 July 2019